DOCTOR · WHO

THE DARKSMITH LEGACY

BBC CHILDREN'S BOOKS
Published by the Penguin Group
Penguin Books Ltd, 80 Strand, London, WC2R 0RL, England
Penguin Group (USA) Inc., 375 Hudson Street, New York 10014, USA
Penguin Books (Australia) Ltd, 250 Camberwell Road, Camberwell, Victoria 3124, Australia
(A division of Pearson Australia Group Pty Ltd)
Canada, India, New Zealand, South Africa
Published by BBC Children's Books, 2009
Text and design © Children's Character Books, 2009
This edition produced for The Book People Ltd,
Hall Wood Avenue, Haydock, St Helens, WA11 9UL
Written by Stephen Cole
Cover illustration by Peter McKinstry
1
ISBN: 9781405906685
Printed in Great Britain by Clays Ltd, St Ives plc

DOCTOR·WHO

THE DARKSMITH LEGACY

THE VAMPIRE OF PARIS

BY STEPHEN COLE

Book
5

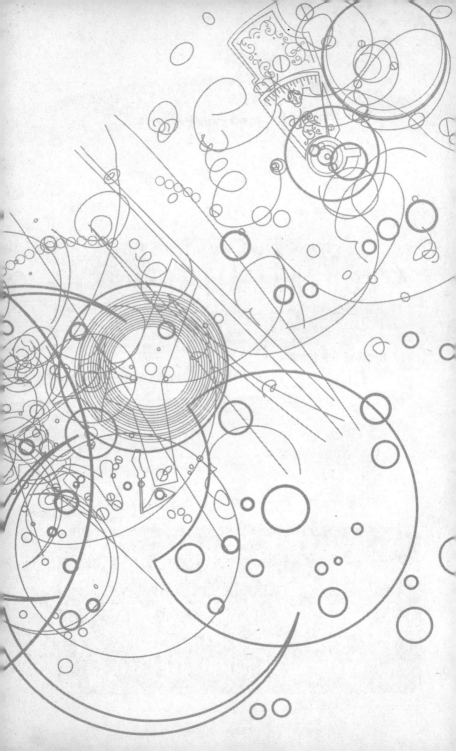

Contents

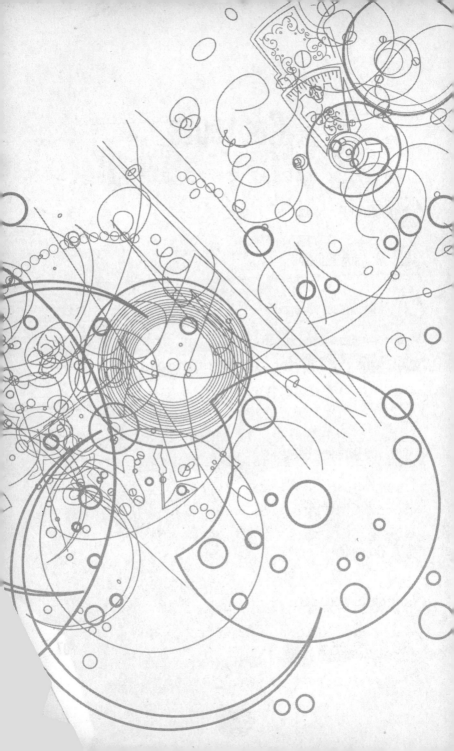

The Story So Far...

The Doctor has taken the powerful Eternity Crystal from the terrible Darksmith Collective on the planet Karagula. The Crystal can create life, and the Doctor knows it mustn't be allowed to fall into the wrong hands.

Varlos, the Darksmith who created the Crystal, realized this too. He stole the Crystal and fled from Karagula. The Darksmiths need the Crystal to fulfil their contract to create a device for a mysterious client. They also need Varlos as he is the only one who really understands how to make the device work. The Doctor wants to find Varlos so he can discover how to destroy the powerful Crystal.

Escaping from a dangerous adventure under water, the Doctor and his friend Gisella, prepare to follow Varlos…

Terror at Midnight

'So where are we going, Gisella?' The Doctor was circling the TARDIS console, a manic bundle of energy and pinstripes jabbing out at the occasional switch and lever. 'Where can we find Varlos, then?'

Gisella was looking round, still in awe and amazement at the impossibly huge room. 'He went to Earth,' she said at last. 'I can give you the exact location.'

'And how would you know that?'

'He was going into retirement. He'd had enough of the Darksmiths and their plotting, scheming ways. He was scared of the Eternity Crystal, terrified of what he had created, and he knew he had to hide it away until he could work out how to destroy it. We managed to escape, and Varlos brought me here.'

The Doctor was surprised. 'You escaped too? From the Darksmiths? All those years ago?'

Gisella nodded. 'Varlos brought me here, to hide me like the Crystal. He wanted me far away, but he wanted the Crystal close enough that he could recover it when he knew how to destroy it.'

'But why would he hide *you*?' The Doctor was confused. 'Who are you, Gisella? Who are you really?'

Gisella sighed. 'I'm sorry Doctor, I really am. But Varlos must have been dead for years. He left me here so long ago, and he was very old even then. I miss him so much. You see – I'm his daughter.'

'Oh,' the Doctor stared. 'Oh Gisella, I'm sorry, I had no idea,' he reflected. 'Mainly because you didn't tell me. I get the feeling there's a lot you're not telling me, Gisella. But look, if you give me the exact location for Varlos, I can sort you out a happy family reunion in no time.'

'Paris,' said Gisella simply. 'The part called Montmartre, in the Earth-relative year 1895.'

The Doctor calculated. '1895, that's going back a bit. You *were* left for a long time, weren't you?' He slammed home the last lever and the TARDIS engines grated noisily into life. The Doctor grinned as Gisella looked around in alarm. 'What? That was a good take-off! Hold on tight!'

As he spoke, the TARDIS lurched – as if something very large had heard his command and thrown its arms around the vessel.

'Is that normal for this craft?' Gisella asked.

'Normal's not a word that goes well with me,' the Doctor admitted, checking some readouts. 'Looks like something's speeding through space and time behind us, riding the TARDIS' coat-tails.' He frowned. 'Or rather, box-tails. Outer plasmic shell-tails. Whatever! They're letting us tow them through the time vortex.'

Gisella frowned. 'They're following us?'

'Trying to. But that's a dodgy business – because unless you know what you're doing, the time winds can spit you back out into reality at a trillion light-years per second…' He winced. 'As whoever was after us has just found out.'

'Who were they?' asked Gisella.

'Dunno,' said the Doctor grimly.

'Dreadbringers?'

The Doctor shook his head. 'They'd be ripped apart in the vortex.'

'Then who?'

'Well, if you see any large dents in nineteenth century Paris, try asking them.' The TARDIS came suddenly to rest. 'Aha! We're here!'

Nicholas rolled over on his hard mattress, listening to the other children snore and snuffle in their sleep. Twenty of them were crammed into one dark room, many squashed together on the hard tiled floor. Madame Misra's orphanage was damp, strict and smelly but it was better than being out on Paris' cobblestones.

A distant clock chimed midnight through the boarded up window.

'Better times are coming,' Nicholas told himself quietly. *In only five years a brand new century will begin, he thought. 1900! I will be fourteen, a proper man. I'll go wherever I choose...*

There was a strange dragging, slithering noise from just outside the room. *SSSCRAPE...*

I'll do whatever I want and no one will be able to stop me.

SSSSSSCRAPE...

The door handle squeaked in the dark as it turned slowly. Nicholas kept his eyes closed.

Madame Misra might cane you if she thought you were awake after candles-out. But what was she carrying? *SSSCRAPE...* He heard the sound again, like a heavy, sticky sack being dragged across the floor.

Then the screaming started.

Nicholas jumped up. The dark dormitory was bathed now in a faint, blood-red glow. Bodies and shadows seemed to mingle in a wild dance of terror as *something* moved through the mass of young boys, lashing out misshapen limbs, snapping inhuman jaws. Nicholas' ears rang with the shrieks of his friends. In a panic he tried to run for the door...

The screams around him were choking off into weird, feeble groans. Nicholas stumbled and fell. He looked up and saw two crimson eyes blazing in a hideous face. As a deformed claw reached out for his neck, Nicholas shrieked loudest of all...

TARDIS
Data Bank

Paris, France

Paris was named after the Parisii tribe who lived in the area from around 250BC. The Romans invaded in 52BC and renamed it Lutetia. But by 400AD towards the end of the Roman occupation its inhabitants called it Paris once more, and it went on to become the capital city of France.

Montmartre

Montmartre (say *mon–MAR–truh*) is the tallest hill in Paris, located in the north of the city. Its name translates as 'Mountain of the Martyr', and is so named because in the third century AD, the Romans made a martyr of the first Bishop of France by killing him on top of the hill. The Romans had built temples to Mars here, and their name for it was *Mons Martis* (Mount of Mars).

The hill was mined extensively in later centuries for gypsum, which is used in making cement. A rabbits' warren of quarries and tunnels lies beneath the surface, as they do beneath much of Paris.

By the end of the nineteenth century, Montmartre had become famous worldwide as a place of new and exciting art movements. Many famous, mould–breaking artists such as Picasso, Van Gogh and Renoir lived here.

'Right, then!' the Doctor yelled. 'Why read about it when you can live it? Come on.' He crossed to the doors and gave Gisella a huge, rakish grin. 'I love Paris, I just love it! *Formidable*! If I were your dad – you know, an alien artisan able to manipulate the raw substance of reality on the run from my own people for stealing a terrifyingly dangerous Crystal of my own creation – I think I'd come here myself. Well, here or Poosh. Can't beat the swimming pools on Poosh. Lovely.' He threw open the doors. 'Go and find Varlos, then, shall we?'

Silently, Gisella followed the Doctor from the control room.

She stepped out into a dark, narrow street. Tall apartment buildings the colour of putty stretched up to the starlit sky, their windows guarded with wooden shutters. The lonely sound of a dog barking somewhere carried faintly across the cobblestones.

'Not as lively as I expected,' the Doctor confessed. 'Where's the partying, the dancing girls? The squabbling artists hitting each other with paintbrushes?'

'It's late,' Gisella observed. 'Everyone must be asleep.'

'Paris doesn't sleep, Montmartre *never* sleeps. Where is everyone?'

Suddenly a hoarse yell sounded from the bottom of the street.

'Maybe we can ask him!' The Doctor sprinted away and Gisella ran after him. Rounding a corner they saw it was an old man who had cried out. He was wrapped in a blanket, standing in front of the window of a small café, clutching his face.

'What's wrong?' asked the Doctor.

'It is impossible,' the old man said throatily, still looking dead ahead. Gisella realized he was looking at his pale, lined reflection in the glass window. 'It can't be true.'

'What?' The Doctor stepped in front of him, all smiles and encouragement. 'You can tell me. I'm the Doctor, this is Gisella. Who are you?'

'My name is Nicholas,' the old man whispered. 'And I am nine years old.'

A Warm Welcome

'Nine?' the Doctor frowned. 'Little closer to *seventy-nine*, I'd say.'

'Please, mister,' Nicholas said, shivering. 'I'm not lying. My orphanage was attacked by... by a *thing*. Dark and slithering and evil. I was a boy of nine when it touched me with its claw, and when it pulled away...' Nicholas lifted his gnarled, wrinkled hand and stared at it in horror. 'Whatever it was, it stole my life and the lives of my friends...'

'He's just a confused old man,' Gisella said quietly. But then she saw that beneath the blanket Nicholas was wearing the torn, grimy remains of a child's nightshirt. 'Isn't he?'

'That would be a nice, easy explanation, wouldn't it?' the Doctor was frowning. 'But I'm a Time Lord. I've got a good nose for time. My nose knows when something's up, and right here, right now in 1895...' He sniffed noisily. 'Not good. Come on, Nicholas!' He grabbed the old man by the arm and led him off down the street. 'Best thing we can do for you is take you to the local nick. The police will check you over – while we check out your story.'

Nicholas nodded but said nothing. He was still staring at his wrinkled hands.

The dim-lit streets were all but empty, and those who braved them flitted past like grim-faced phantoms.

But the little police station stood in stark contrast. 'Noisiest place in town,' the Doctor noted. A crowd of old people were huddled up on the floor just outside, with many more jostling in the smoky confines of the station room itself. Gisella overheard two French policemen talking quietly to themselves.

'Tell me how an orphanage can become an old person's home overnight?' the first complained.

'Only if you tell me how the animals of the Circus Fernando can age to old bones between performances?' the second shook his head gravely. 'Inspector DuPont is going crazy back there in his office. I tell you, a devil's curse has befallen Paris.'

'Well, it's one theory, boys,' said the Doctor brightly, pulling out his psychic paper. 'I'm Divisional Commissioner Doctor LeSmith, Ministry of the Interior. Here to help you sort things out.'

The two policemen jumped to attention. 'Forgive us, sir,' said the first. 'We did not know you were coming.'

'Expect the unexpected, officer.' The Doctor eyed the confused old men slumped against the wall. 'And get these poor people somewhere warm and dry and give them hot drinks, can't you see they're in shock?' he raised his voice. 'Wake up the neighbours, get those kettles on. Go on, get on your bikes!'

Wincing, the policemen hurried to obey.

'How do I understand the local language?' Gisella wondered. 'It's like… I can feel a presence in my— my brain. Something taking the sounds I hear and twisting them into words I understand…'

'The TARDIS can translate any language,' the Doctor announced, watching her closely. 'Though not many people can feel it working. You must have an exceptional mind, Gisella.'

She looked uncomfortable and glanced away.

'Thank you.'

'I thank you too, Doctor,' said Nicholas. 'For believing me.' The Doctor stared sadly at the doddery old men. 'These old wrecks were boys like me just hours ago. How can it be?'

'I'm going to find out,' the Doctor promised. 'Stay with your friends. Help them if you can. I'll find you later.'

The Doctor pushed into the crowded station and waggled his fingers at the harassed clerk behind the desk. 'Doctor LeSmith, from the Ministry, blah-blah-blah. DuPont in his office round the back, is he? Burning the midnight oil again! Won't he be glad to see me, eh?'

'Inspector DuPont already has an advisor, sir,' said a gravelly voice behind him. 'And I am he.'

The Doctor turned to face a tall, lean man with dark, thinning hair, dressed in a dark, starched suit. His face was craggy and florid red. He wore a patch over one eye; the other glittered keenly in the light of the oil lamp as the Doctor held up his psychic paper for inspection. 'And you would be…?'

'Baron De Guerre.' He turned to Gisella and his gaze hardened. 'You allow a young girl to accompany you at such a dark hour?'

'She's older than she looks,' the Doctor assured her. 'Actually, she's *my* advisor. You can never have too many advisors at a time like this, can you? Now, where's DuPont, eh? Lead the way. *Allons y!*'

'You speak Welsh!' cried an old man on the floor.

'Happens every time,' the Doctor sighed. 'Come *on*.'

Inspector DuPont looked away from his files and rubbed his puffy eyes. He was a portly man in his mid-fifties, and he was tired. Not only because he'd been up all night – that was a regular event these days. DuPont was tired of feeling helpless while an unknown menace roamed the streets of Paris, hurting, ruining or destroying all those he touched with devilish, unnatural powers.

He looked at the street map of Montmartre pinned to his wall – at the growing number of red crosses that marred its narrow, winding paths – and wondered if the horror would ever end.

There was a sudden knock at his door and Baron De Guerre ushered in a young, smiling man in a pinstripe suit and a dark-haired girl. DuPont sighed. They looked like a bad cabaret act from some ghastly showplace like the Moulin Rouge.

'I'm the Doctor, this is Gisella, we're—'

'I heard you talking outside,' DuPont interrupted. 'So, I am to have more advisors, yes? More cooks spoiling the broth?'

'We aren't chefs,' said Gisella, baffled.

'But you're certainly in the soup, aren't you, Inspector,' said the Doctor quietly. 'Maybe we can help. Why not show me those files of yours?'

DuPont wearily passed him the top page. 'Advise me on this, LeSmith, if you're so clever. How many years from the lives of these good citizens have been stolen by this demon of the night – this *vampire* of Paris?'

Activity

Name	Age	Estimated age now
Henri D'Estaing	22	85
Philippe Buffet	17	90
Charlotte Aubrac	34	76
Violette Chaban	16	90
Pierre La Brasse	25	70
Geraldine De Villiers	19	100
Madeleine Misra	56	2

Calculating stolen years...

Answer: _____

The Doctor took the paper. A moment later he responded: 'A total of 378 years have been taken from six young victims, catapulting them into old age…'

Gisella stood on tiptoes to look too. 'But there's no pattern, even allowing for rough age estimates… And the victims aren't only aging – one's been made younger!'

'432 years missing, all told,' the Doctor concluded. 'Only that's *not* all told, is it? That's just the tip of the iceberg. Just the ones you know about. Even our new friend Nicholas isn't on this list yet.'

'Madame Misra ran the orphanage where most of the old men outside used to live,' announced De Guerre. 'An infant in woman's clothing was found crawling outside the building. It was only later we realized that the orphanage itself had been attacked…'

'This dark, slithering thing our friend Nicholas saw…' The Doctor grabbed the file from the desk and started riffling through it. 'You called it a vampire, DuPont – a figure of speech, I know, but you're actually not far off. Only this thing doesn't suck the blood from its victims, it feeds on time itself. Pure, temporal energy.'

DuPont stared at him. 'This is no jesting matter, Doctor.'

'That's why I'm not jesting,' the Doctor's eyes held the inspector's own. 'I've come across chronovores before, devourers of time. But trust me, a chronovore could destroy a whole continent in ten minutes. It wouldn't feed on scraps night after night like this creature. This is something else.' The Doctor slammed the file down on the desk. 'It doesn't even seem bothered by who or what it targets, does it? Young people, old people, circus animals even…'

'Which makes it hard to predict what it will do next,' Gisella agreed.

'And which is why the killer has not yet been caught,' De Guerre nodded to the street map. 'But his main place of operations is here in Montmartre. We *must* find him soon…'

'Then we'd best get walking the beat like good policemen,' said the Doctor. 'I've got some equipment in, er, one of those new-fangled police boxes down the way. I'm guessing our time vampire must leave temporally distorted molecules in its wake.'

Gisella nodded. 'You mean like a trail of time decay?'

'Right!' the Doctor grinned. 'We can get following

the thing, and then get on with the real business of finding old Varlos.'

Exasperated, DuPont turned to De Guerre. 'Are you following this, Baron?'

'Not one word,' De Guerre replied coldly, his good eye fixed on the Doctor. 'But I feel I should accompany you.'

'What, so the advisor can advise the other advisor and *his* advisor?' The Doctor raised his eyebrows. 'Is that advisable?'

'It is happening, Doctor LeSmith,' De Guerre said flatly as he opened the door. 'Let us go.'

The shadowy streets of Montmartre were still mostly empty. The Doctor strode through them, ahead of De Guerre and Gisella, his hands deep in the pockets of his long brown coat. He could detect a strange tension in the air, an unearthly presence close by. The time vampire? Or something else…

'You wait with his lordship,' the Doctor told Gisella as they neared the street where the TARDIS had arrived. 'I'll just fetch our, er, equipment.'

He jogged a hundred metres or so down the darkened road and a sickly burning smell reached his nostrils. 'Burnt out strontium circuits?' the Doctor frowned. 'In 1895?'

Then a large man-shaped figure, its scarred pitted body gleaming in the moonlight, appeared from behind the TARDIS. Part burnt metal, part scorched and blackened plastic, the figure stepped forward to confront him, its white eyes shining like the stars.

The Doctor recognised it in a double heartbeat – the robotic Agent sent by the Darksmiths to execute Varlos and take back the Eternity Crystal. The fact that the Doctor now owned the Crystal simply meant that the Agent had added him to its list of targets for destruction.

'It was you who followed the TARDIS through the vortex,' the Doctor realized. 'You must have been on the Dreadbringers' ship back on Despair. You followed the TARDIS when we escaped, and you were almost destroyed.'

'There was a puncture in the fabric of space-and-time in the vicinity of your landing point,' the robot droned. 'I found my way through.'

'But at what cost,' the Doctor muttered. 'Look at you. You're in a bad way.'

'My destructive capability is unimpaired,' the

Agent assured him, pointing its right fist at the Doctor's head. 'Observe.'

A blinding force beam spat from its knuckles…

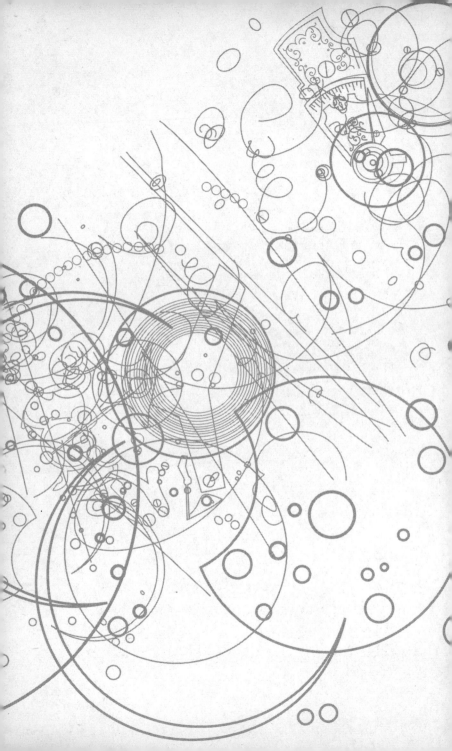

The Streets of Fear

The Doctor had barely a split second to react. It wasn't enough. He fell back, cracking his head on the cobblestones…

Then he realized with some surprise that he was still alive – while the Agent had collapsed back against the TARDIS, smoke gusting from its right arm.

'Power siphons damaged in re-entry.' The Agent's voice knifed through the silence of the night. 'Force-beam dispersed prematurely. Effect: non-lethal.'

The Doctor grinned weakly. 'Your gun jammed!'

'Clearing blockage.' The Agent inserted a complex tool into its scorched arm.

'Your logic circuits must be blocked too.' The Doctor struggled up onto all fours. 'Why kill me before you know where I've hidden the Crystal?'

'My bio-sensors have detected the presence of Varlos in this area,' the Agent informed him. 'Also that of the Gisella entity he sought to protect.'

'She's a girl, not an entity!' the Doctor snapped.

'Logic dictates Varlos has the means to track the Crystal. If I threaten the Gisella entity's death, he will obey me prior to his own execution.'

'Got it all worked out, haven't you?' The Doctor prepared to summon all his strength for a sudden sprint. The robot would soon clear the blockage and fire again, but the damage to its legs hopefully meant it couldn't chase him far. The most important thing was to put some cover between him and the Agent's blaster.

He glanced around the silent street and tried to work out an escape route, knowing that the fastest way might not necessarily be the safest.

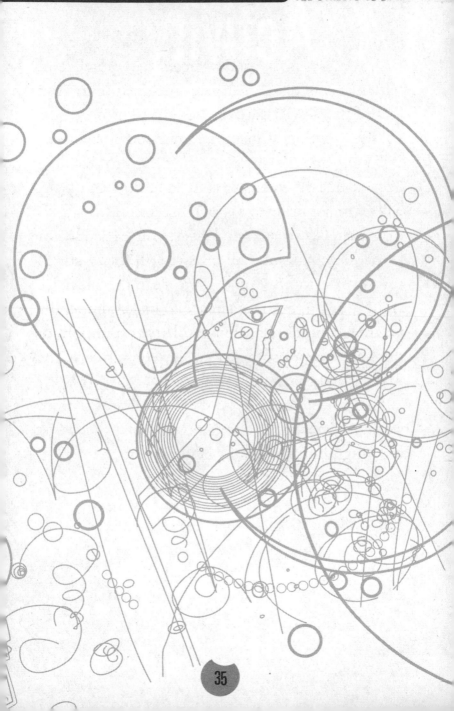

Activity

Which route should the Doctor take?

Key

 The Doctor

 The Robot

 The Tardis

 Rubbish

 Stall

 Fountain

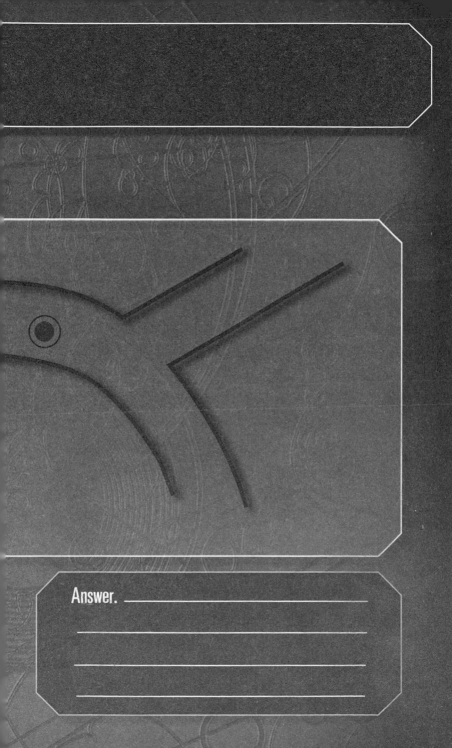

Answer.

'Now or never,' the Doctor muttered, scrambling to his feet and resolving to use all the cover he could. He dashed for a closed up tobacconist's stall across the street. Just as he hurled himself behind it, a searing blast of light struck the pavement close by, showering him with stone shards. He hurtled off again, diving for cover in a pile of rotting garbage. Another blast from the robotic Agent – the rubbish was blown sky-high, and the Doctor nearly with it. Finally he dashed out of sight into the next street, the thin soles of his trainers slapping hard on the cobbles as he raced to find Gisella and De Guerre.

But the street where he'd left them was deserted.

'Doctor!' The cry was faint and some way off, but it was Gisella's, no question. The Doctor set off again, a pinstriped shadow flying through the Parisian night. He tore up a steep staircase. The ghostly white dome of a massive church hovered over the rooftops like a gigantic second moon, lighting his way. Then, panting for breath, he emerged onto a boulevard and found two huddled figures crouched beside a third.

'What took you so long?' demanded De Guerre.

'Trouble with an old friend.' The Doctor

frowned as he saw the skeleton sprawled on the cobblestones.

'It's horrible, Doctor. Horrible.' Gisella looked up at him, her eyes brimming with tears. 'We heard a cry while you were gone, and though we came quickly… This was all that was left.' She wiped her eyes. 'The bones are more like chalk. A complete cellular collapse.'

The Doctor nodded. 'As if every last drop of time had been sucked out of the corpse. Our vampire is a messy eater.'

'There is not enough of this poor woman left to be identified even by dental records.' De Guerre's voice was shot through with anger and sorrow. 'I hope this equipment of yours will bring swift results, Doctor LeSmith?'

'Couldn't get it. Trouble with the lock. Try again tomorrow.' To Gisella, he mouthed 'Darksmith robot!' and her eyes widened with shock. 'The robot Agent is too weak after its journey through the vortex to chase after us right now,' the Doctor whispered. 'But it'll be fixing itself up as we speak. It needs you in order to get at Varlos… and it said something about a puncture in the fabric of space-and-time close by.' He rubbed the back of his neck.

'Could be how this time vampire got access to Earth. Maybe Varlos, too. Their both being here in Paris can't be just coincidence.'

Gisella nodded. 'Perhaps if we solve one mystery we'll get at the other. If the Agent – or the vampire – let us live that long…'

Even as she spoke, the skeleton crumbled into dust and blew away along the gutters of the boulevard.

'Cease your mutterings,' rasped De Guerre, getting up stiffly. 'It will soon be dawn. This monster has never attacked in daylight.' He sounded tired, but his voice still rang with a cold fury. 'Let us return to my apartment, there is a telephone there. I shall inform DuPont of this incident. It seems it is all we can do, for now.'

'For now,' the Doctor agreed. 'But we're going to find this vampire, De Guerre. And we're going to stop it.' He watched the dust spiral away into the darkness. 'Make no bones about that.'

De Guerre's apartment was grand but tired-looking. A lifetime's worth of possessions seemed crammed into its few rooms, most of them covered in dust.

'Been a while since you had the maid in, my

lord,' the Doctor noted.

De Guerre ignored him. 'Gisella, you may sleep in my study. Doctor, I can offer you only the floor of my sitting room.'

'Lovely,' the Doctor smiled. 'Night, then.'

Once De Guerre had retired to his bedroom, the Doctor had a good nose through the jumble of possessions. In an unlocked drawer, he found a bleary, sepia photo of a younger De Guerre, marked *Tunisia, 1880*. There the old boy stood with his eye-patch, and a bunch of soldiers. There was a small bundle of pictures of a young lady dressed as a dancer, tied with red ribbon – a lost love, perhaps. A bureau stood half buried beneath all sorts of official papers. The Doctor noted a wad of fifty Franc notes, a cheque book, title deeds to an apartment in the posh Place Vendôme, even a warm letter from Napoleon III, the former ruler of France, praising De Guerre's conduct in the Crimean War.

The Doctor half-suspected the old man knew more about this whole business than he was letting on. But everything in the apartment seemed to check out as legitimate, and he supposed it was hardly surprising that a local war hero of such stature and influence would help the police in such a serious, sensitive matter.

He was about to put his feet up on the sofa and close his eyes when, in the corner of the room beneath a table, he noticed an old, wooden chest secured with a padlock. 'He leaves his valuables out in plain sight... so what does he keep in the trunk, his dirty washing?' the Doctor grinned and got out the sonic screwdriver. 'Ooh, I love locked boxes...'

But suddenly the shrill clamour of an upright telephone shattered the silence. The Doctor bounded over crossly and snatched up the little receiver on its piece of twisted flex. 'Yes? D'you know what time it is?' he complained.

'This is DuPont.' There was an edge of excitement to the faint, crackling voice. 'Is that you, LeSmith? You must tell De Guerre – our vampire's been sighted, close to the Tower!'

'The Eiffel Tower?' the Doctor frowned. 'But that's clear across Paris!'

'The military police have been summoned,' DuPont went on. 'They'll soon have him surrounded. We've got him, LeSmith – we've got him!'

Beast of the Tower

'Listen to me, DuPont,' the Doctor commanded. 'No one approaches that creature till I get there – got it?'

'A carriage is on its way to collect you,' said DuPont. 'I am leaving now.'

The phone went dead. At the same moment, DeGuerre emerged from his room and Gisella burst from hers, both dressed and ready.

'The vampire's been sighted?' De Guerre demanded.

Gisella looked at him. 'I thought you said it never came out in daylight?'

'It has never aged people to dust or reduced grown women to babies before either,' the old man said.

'Where's that carriage,' the Doctor fretted.

TARDIS
Data Bank

The Eiffel Tower

Known in France as *le Tour Eiffel*, the Eiffel Tower was constructed between 1887 and 1889 in the *Champ-de-Mars* (Field of Mars) area close to the River Seine. Until 1930, it was the tallest building in the world. But even today it is the tallest building in Paris, and famous around the world as a symbol of France.

The tower was assembled from 18,038 pieces of iron held together by two-and-a-half million rivets, as part of the celebrations to mark one hundred years since the French Revolution. However, many people in Paris disliked the tower enormously, thinking it an ugly eyesore. At first, the tower was only meant to stand for twenty years and was due to be demolished in 1909. But once hooked up to long-range transmitters, the tower proved useful for radio communications and was allowed to remain standing.

Every seven years it is covered in fifty to sixty tonnes of paint to prevent it from rusting; three shades of paint are used — the lightest at the top and the darkest at the bottom — so the tower seems a uniform colour to spectators on the ground.

'We must get to the Eiffel Tower, pronto. On the double. Now!'

The police carriage thundered along the Rue Tronchet, the racket of its rattling wheels was rivalled only by the clopping hooves of the horses that pulled it.

Gisella sat between De Guerre and the Doctor in the covered carriage. 'What are you planning, Doctor?' she shouted over the noise. 'How can you stop something that sucks the time out of people?'

'I'll try conversation to start with,' the Doctor shrugged. 'If we can understand what it's doing, what its motives are—'

'Its motives are to destroy,' De Guerre countered. 'We must send it back to where it came from.'

The Doctor turned to him. 'And just where exactly *did* it come from?'

De Guerre met his gaze, but did not reply.

'Up until now the creature has stayed around Montmartre,' Gisella mused, as their carriage ploughed through the wide-open sweep of the Place de la Concorde. 'Why would it suddenly shift across the river, so far from its base?'

'Perhaps we'll soon see,' said the Doctor, steeling himself for action. The fat grey stripe of the Seine had come into view, as serene and dull as the dawn sky overhead. 'We're nearly there.'

The Eiffel Tower dwarfed the buildings and trees around it, rising up like a great iron scaffold to the sky. Figures in dark uniform circled it on police horses, surrounding the vast four-pronged base of the tower.

The Doctor noticed Gisella's puzzled look. 'They're gendarmes, France's military police,' he explained. 'The four-legged things are horses. And look, there's old DuPont.'

DuPont was standing in a small crowd of policemen, staring intently up at the Tower through binoculars. The Doctor caught movement on the Tower's second level – a glimpse of darkness between the stitchwork of girders. He ran over to join the inspector.

'That ridiculous Tower,' DuPont grumbled. 'We ought to bring it down on that monster's head— *urgh*!'

The Doctor had grabbed DuPont's binoculars, half-strangling him with the neck strap, and squinted through them. A ferocious, bestial face and black, matted hair flashed into focus.

'Keep everyone back,' the Doctor told DuPont.

'I'm going up there – alone.'

'But you can't,' DuPont protested. 'It has blocked off the staircase to the second observation platform with metal torn from the first – its strength is hideous!'

'Its face isn't much to write home about either,' the Doctor commented. 'Don't worry, I'll scale the outside.'

'Wait!' Gisella caught up with him. 'Let me come with you!'

De Guerre marched up behind her and took hold of her hand. 'No, my child. You will stay here where it is safer.'

'I'm *not* a child!' Gisella retorted. 'Tell him, Doctor.'

'He's right, though,' the Doctor said, with a level glance at De Guerre. 'You will be safer down here. I'll see you soon.' He gazed up at the tower and gulped. 'Blimey, I hate climbing towers…'

He ran off towards the massive iron sprawl of the Tower's base. Using the girders as though they were giant rungs for the mother of all ladders, he climbed athletically upwards, his long coat flapping around him in the stiff morning breeze. His arms and legs soon ached with the effort of scaling the metal links, and he was grateful for the purchase the many rivets gave him. Before too long he was a dizzying height above the ground – and his climb was blocked by a two-metre overhang above his head. Taking a deep breath, he lunged for the lip of metal, found handholds and painfully began to pull himself up and over…

DuPont waited tensely while Gisella followed the Doctor's progress through the binoculars. 'Just how high up is that observation platform?' she asked.

'One hundred and fifteen metres,' De Guerre reported. 'He's got barely twenty five metres to go.'

'If he falls, he's dead,' grumbled DuPont. 'And if he makes it as far as that monster he'll be dead too.'

'That thing can't know he's scaling the outside of the tower,' said Gisella. 'He'll have the element of surprise.'

'He'll need more than that,' said De Guerre quietly. 'How did you come to meet him, Gisella?'

'We're on a kind of quest…' She lowered the binoculars, biting her lip. 'I don't think you'd understand.'

'Even the old have their quests,' said De Guerre quietly.

The wind howled eerily through the thick iron struts of the Eiffel Tower as the Doctor finally hauled himself parallel to the second platform. The creature was facing away from him. It was squat and hugely powerful, more like an ape than a man. With a frown, the Doctor saw tatters of clothing clinging to its dark, hairy form. 'Blue overalls,' the Doctor murmured, stringing his way carefully and quietly through the angled girders.

He was about to drop down onto the platform, when the creature seemed to sense him and whirled round, fangs bared, snarling.

The Doctor froze. 'I only want to talk. *Can* you talk?'

The monster cocked its head to one side, as if puzzled by the way the Doctor hung from the iron rafters. It bellowed, and thumped its muscular chest with one fist.

'Yep, you're stronger than I am,' the Doctor said quickly. 'I'm not arguing, but I need to know – why all the killings? Do you even know what you're doing?' The monster growled. 'Can you communicate at all?'

With one hand still clenched in a fist, the monster wrenched a length of iron lattice away from the arch above it and swung it furiously like a club. The Doctor dropped to the platform deck to avoid it, but landed awkwardly. He couldn't dodge a savage kick from the ape-like foot that sent him sprawling into the safety barrier. In a daze, he saw the thing stamp towards him, frothing at the mouth.

The monster grabbed the Doctor by the neck with one hand and swung him as easily as a stuffed dummy over the edge of the platform parapet. The Doctor saw a blur of the Paris skyline, glimpsed a scattering of blue-clad figures below, heard the thunderous crack of rifle shots and gasped as he was hurled through empty space.

Bare Bones

The Doctor woke with a terrible pounding in his ears. He realized it was the horses again, their steel-shod hooves cracking on the cobbles. He was back in the police carriage, hurtling through Paris.

Gisella was beside him, clutching his hand. 'Are you all right? Any double vision? Nausea? Migraine? Amnesia? Loss of sensation?'

'Earache,' said the Doctor wryly.

'You were knocked out cold. We're on our way to the hospital,' Gisella told him, 'in case you need treatment.'

'I'm fine.' He rubbed his head, still sore from his run-in with the Agent, and winced. 'That creature. What happened?'

'The vampire was about to throw you off the Tower – so one of the gendarmes shot it. It dropped you as it fell – you landed back on the platform, luckily.'

'That thing *wasn't* the vampire,' the Doctor sat up with a groan. 'I'm sure of it.'

'Well, DuPont is certain that it *is*,' said Gisella. 'He told the gendarmes it was an escaped zoo animal. The body's been brought back to the cells in secret, and De Guerre is going to use his contacts to make sure the truth never comes out. The people of Montmartre will be celebrating tonight. As far as they're concerned, the threat is over.'

'I doubt that.'

Gisella looked puzzled. 'But that thing was a monster. If not the vampire—'

'There are all kinds of monsters,' the Doctor reminded her. 'I mean, look at old Varlos. You could say that conjuring life from death for profit makes *him* a monster, in a way.'

Gisella took her hand from his. 'My father tried to make amends for what he did. He wanted to destroy the Crystal.'

'But what if something went wrong? And what if the time vampire is here as a result?' The Doctor leaned his sore head out of the carriage window. 'Oi! Driver! Forget the hospital, take us to the police station in Montmartre! *Allons y!*'

'What was that Welsh bit, sir?' the driver called back.

'Blimey,' the Doctor muttered. 'Whenever I speak in the local lingo it comes out as Welsh. But maybe if I try Welsh…' He cleared his throat. 'All right – *dewlch ymlaen!*'

'Ah!' The driver touched his hand to his cap. 'Yes, I'll get going there, don't worry.'

The Doctor grinned at Gisella. 'Don't you just love travelling? Always something new to discover!'

The cell was lit with two flickering candles, almost like a chapel of rest for the inhuman body on the floor. The moment the Doctor walked in, Gisella saw him nod to himself. 'Poor thing,' he murmured, crouching beside it. 'This should never have happened.'

Gisella heard movement behind her and turned to see Nicholas, the nine-year-old pensioner, standing in the doorway. His face was a sad maze of deep lines and wrinkles. 'That's not the thing that attacked me,' he said. 'Sure, it's dark enough. But the vampire was bigger, it slithered. And its eyes…'

He shuddered. 'This is something else.'

'You're sure?' asked Gisella.

'*I* am.' The Doctor pulled a scrap of paper from the creature's fist and scanned it. 'Look – the employment card for one Pierre Breton. He lived in Montmartre, but worked at the Tower.'

'Blue overalls,' Nicholas whispered, pointing at the bloodied scraps around the beast's waist. 'Yes, I've seen the cleaners at the Tower wear them.'

'The monster could have taken these things as trophies,' Gisella argued.

'Poor old Pierre *is* the monster,' said the Doctor. 'The vampire must have transformed him into an earlier stage of human evolution, millions of years back. The Missing Link, if you like.'

Gisella was baffled. 'But this thing's been devouring time measured in decades. How can it revert somebody through millions of years of evolution?'

'Most likely answer is that our vampire is cloaked in some kind of protective time shield,' said the Doctor, 'designed to contain the energy it leaches from its victims—'

'But the shield is not working right,' Nicholas

suggested. 'It keeps … misfiring?'

The Doctor grinned. 'Oh, Nicholas, you're very good! Misfiring, that's the word. Last night Gisella and I saw the creature age bones to dust in a second, when bones can endure for millions of years.' He gestured at the bestial corpse at their feet. 'And this morning… it does this.'

'I see,' Nicholas murmured.

Gisella was surprised. 'You accept these things?'

'He's got the opposite problem to you. There's the mind of a nine-year-old in that body,' the Doctor reminded her. 'Best minds around. Anything's possible! Well, except convincing DuPont that his problems – and Montmartre's – are far from over. That'll be hopeless. He'll be on a high, busy sweeping everything under the carpet.'

'Well, he's not sweeping me under the carpet,' said Nicholas firmly. 'What's happened to me mustn't happen to anyone else. If we can only talk to Baron De Guerre, convince him he's made a mistake…'

'Then perhaps he can convince DuPont,' Gisella agreed.

'Well, you're our star witness where the vampire's concerned, Nicholas,' said the Doctor. 'Shall we go?'

Soon Nicholas, Gisella and the Doctor were clattering in the police carriage over to De Guerre's apartment. A calm seemed to have fallen over Montmartre. The picturesque streets were warmed by the afternoon sunlight, and the breeze ruffled trees heavy with lilac spears. News of apparent victory over the menace must have already spread among the locals, for there were busy, boisterous crowds at the bars and cafés, and much clinking of glasses as rosy futures were toasted.

'I had so many plans for my life,' Nicholas said, gazing out of the window. 'I would sneak off here some nights, walk past the cafés and dance halls, and dream of belonging. I couldn't wait to be older...' He sighed wistfully. 'You see, here is a place where the people help each other, support each other. Artists and writers, thinkers, comedians and dancing girls...'

'That's it! That's what's been bugging me!' The Doctor sat up bolt upright on the wooden seat. 'How does a straight-laced old baron with an apartment on the posh side of town wind up over here in the company of brilliant dropouts and penniless artisans?'

'Perhaps he felt like a change,' said Gisella.

'Perhaps,' the Doctor considered. 'Old Varlos would've liked it here, wouldn't he? A master craftsman but radical and unconventional. No wonder he thought he would fit in here.'

Gisella sighed. 'The vampire might already have made him a victim. Or the Agent, for all we know. We might never find Varlos. But the Agent will find us…'

'Agent?' Nicholas echoed. 'Like an actor's agent?'

'This one's after a bit more than ten per cent of our cash,' said the Doctor. 'The streets tonight, Nicholas, will be more dangerous than ever. What's taking this carriage so long?'

At last the driver slowed the horses outside De Guerre's residence, and his passengers piled outside. 'Hello?' the Doctor hollered as he dashed up the steps to the Baron's first floor apartment. When there was no reply he buzzed the sonic screwdriver to the front door, which jumped open. 'Hold the front page! You're…' He looked around frantically. 'You're…'

'Gone,' Gisella concluded.

Still wheezing from the climb up the stairs, Nicholas picked up a coffee mug. 'This is still warm,' he reported, and slurped down the dregs with a satisfied sigh. 'He hasn't been gone long.'

'But he *has* been at his trunk.' The Doctor pointed to the old wooden chest. It had been dragged out from beneath the table in the corner, and the heavy chains disturbed. 'Hmm. Now, obviously I don't approve of breaking and entering...'

'We just broke into his house!' Gisella reminded him.

'Yeah, but did you hear one word of approval?' A blur of blue light from the sonic screwdriver and the chains fell away. Gisella and Nicholas leaned in as the Doctor opened the chest...

The technology inside meant nothing to Nicholas – broken shards of wired-up crystal, weird metal tools, crazy objects from a fiction-writer's fancy. But Gisella gasped out loud, her dark eyes wide with shock. 'The tools of a Darksmith,' she breathed. 'These belong to Varlos, I know it.'

The Doctor shifted some of the scientific clutter – and froze.

Beneath the bric-a-brac lay a bundle of bleached white bones. A skull stared up at them from the top of the pile, fragments of crystal glittering in the dark sockets.

Nicholas gulped. 'Do those belong to Varlos too?'

Gisella burst into shuddering sobs. The Doctor rose to comfort her, but she pulled away and stood alone near the window. 'It seems you were right, Doctor.' She wiped furiously at her eyes. 'In coming here, in trying to destroy the Crystal, Varlos *did* unleash a terror onto this world.' Hugging herself, she turned away to the window. 'And he's paid the price.'

'So it must be De Guerre!' Nicholas said slowly. '*He's* the time vampire! He got involved in this case to mislead the police, not to help them!'

'If that's true, then the sixty-four million Franc question is – why didn't he kill us while we were kipping here last night?' The Doctor stared down at the trunk broodingly. 'And what's he planning now?' He crouched and carefully sifted through the scientific odds and ends in the trunk. 'You know, with a little more equipment like this I could make one of those vampire-trackers I told you about, trace that trail of time-decay he must leave in his wake. Of course, carrying out-of-place technology will make it easier for the Agent to track *us* down, but—'

'Doctor!' Gisella had stiffened at the window. 'Doctor, it already has. It's found us. The Agent is here!'

The Darkness Beneath

The Doctor dashed over to the window. Sure enough, outside in the street stood the Agent. It had covered itself with a threadbare blanket, but there was no disguising its bulk or its awkward, robotic gait. People in the street pointed and laughed, thinking it was some crazy piece of new art, or an escaped prop from a cabaret show, never guessing the danger they were in, or its sinister purpose in approaching De Guerre's apartment.

'It hasn't completely repaired itself then,' the Doctor muttered. 'But it just couldn't wait to get started.'

'It's a thing of clockwork?' asked Nicholas.

'Killer clockwork,' the Doctor informed him.

'And it's after us?'

'Afraid so.'

'No, wait. It's going away!' Gisella marvelled as she watched the Agent shuffle past their doorway and head further along the street, heedless of the heckles and catcalls at its passing. 'But why? It's searching for us.'

'And Varlos,' the Doctor realized, still sorting through the chest. 'Keeping its sensors peeled for super-advanced extraterrestrials on this primitive planet. So how does he track us? Through our technology emissions!' He looked down at the tools in his hand and suddenly dropped them on the carpet. 'Someone else must be using louder gadgets than the sonic screwdriver. De Guerre, of course – carrying Darksmith technology he took from the trunk…' The Doctor jumped up and sprinted to the door. 'Come on, then!'

Nicholas looked baffled. 'You want us to go after that clockwork killer?'

Gisella shook her head. 'He wants us to go after De Guerre – and if the Agent can track him…'

'Then we can track the Agent,' the Doctor agreed. 'Very, very carefully.'

Nicholas sighed. It was difficult, wanting to move

like a nine-year-old when you had the bones of someone sixty years older. But though his body was tired and aching, Nicholas couldn't bring himself to give up. After all, the time vampire had made some of its victims younger, hadn't it? If there was a chance that Nicholas could become a child again… well, he'd risk anything to take it.

The Doctor seemed no stranger to risk. His idea of careful tracking was to stride noisily from bar to bar, drinking coffee and swapping banter with anyone who'd listen.

'We're trying to fit in,' he explained to Nicholas and Gisella, when they proved reluctant to join in as heartily. 'By now, the robot must be used to humans being noisy and having fun, so that's not suspicious behaviour as far as its sensors are concerned. But if it picks up on three sets of stealthy footsteps creeping up in silence…'

Gisella grabbed an empty cup from a nearby table and pretended to drink. 'Oh, that's so good!' she shouted.

Nicholas lifted an abandoned glass of beer but the Doctor snatched it from his lips. 'You're too young,' he said, confusing the nearby customers.

Onwards they went, up through the winding

Sacred Heart

The white-domed Basilica of the Sacre Coeur (say *SACK-ra KUR*) is a famous place of worship, towering at the summit of Montmartre's hill. Its name means 'Sacred Heart'. Building began in 1876 but would not finish until 1912. In 1895 it was the second-tallest structure in Paris, with only the Eiffel Tower standing taller.

streets and steep staircases of Montmartre. The bars and cafes grew fewer, the crowds thinned out. Nicholas was quaking with fear even as he made out he was having the time of his life.

Dominating the skyline above was a huge, magnificent, spotless white building still under construction. Scaffolding clung to the vast domes and turrets, timbers and other building materials lay littered all around. It was as if a fairy tale castle was being built, a place of dreams, and yet the low drone of chanting voices reminded Nicholas that this was a church.

'The Agent seems to be headed for the Sacre Coeur,' said the Doctor.

'What is it?' Gisella wondered.

The Doctor rattled off a quick lesson.

'Why would De Guerre go to such a place?' said Gisella.

'Perhaps he hasn't.' The Doctor held up a warning hand, as ahead of them the Agent abruptly left the pavement and headed towards a temporary shelter set up by the construction workers on the muddy hillside. It disappeared inside through a doorway of old sacking. Nicholas joined the Doctor and Gisella down a small side street and braced himself for the screams of those inside.

None came. A few minutes later, the Agent re-emerged. The Doctor and his companions shrank back as it climbed doggedly with its damaged legs further up the hillside.

'What's it looking for?' the Doctor murmured. 'Why go cross-country?'

'Let's look in that shelter.' Gisella ran nimbly across with the Doctor, while Nicholas stumbled along behind.

Save for a table, some old oil lamps and a few boxes of building supplies, the shelter seemed empty. 'The Agent wouldn't have come here if De Guerre didn't go in first,' the Doctor decided. 'So where is he now?'

Nicholas felt a draft around his ankles and shivered. He hated the way his stick-thin body played up at the tiniest excuse, and looked around for the source of the draft. It seemed to be coming from behind a panel of wood set into the back of the shelter. 'But the back is set against the hillside...' he muttered, and pulled at the wood.

The Doctor noticed what he was doing and came to help. The wood came away – to reveal a crack in the rock, just wide enough for a man to climb through.

'Nicholas, you found it!' the Doctor grinned. 'Of course, De Guerre must have come in and sneaked through the gap. The Agent knew it was way too big to have a hope of following so it pushed off looking for another way in.'

Gisella frowned. '*Into* the hillside?'

'Remember the TARDIS data bank? What it said about Montmartre?' The Doctor was already peering into the split in the rock. 'This hill was mined hard for centuries; it's like Swiss cheese now on the inside. Hardly surprising if the excavations for the Sacre Coeur exposed some of the old mine openings.'

Nicholas nodded and started to light one of the oil lamps. 'I heard that the quarrymen tried to prop up the spent mines with columns of stone when they left. It would be a very good place to hide something…'

The Doctor nodded. 'But what, eh? What?'

Gisella lit a lamp of her own, and was first to clamber through the fissure. 'Let's stop talking, and find out!'

A cold, dank passageway waited on the other

side of the fissure. The Doctor helped Nicholas through, then took the lead. Nicholas and Gisella followed just behind him. No sun had ever warmed these rocky walls, and Nicholas could feel the chill creeping into his brittle bones as he walked, clutching his own lamp in one hand and Gisella's hand in the other.

The tunnel curved. Then, as if the rock itself was yawning, the passage grew slowly wider around them. It opened onto an enormous cavern – the slightest sound echoed over and over, and the darkness seemed thicker than ever.

'Wait…' Gisella started forwards, her keen eyes sighting something ahead of them. 'What's that?'

The Doctor raised his lamp like a charm to ward off the shadows, and his low whistle sounded spookily through the gloom. 'You'd know better than me, Gisella. But I think it's a Darksmith spaceship.'

Nicholas could hardly believe his fading eyes. A large, intricate structure like a cathedral in miniature stood ahead of them, carved from pale-coloured rock. Veins of strange minerals ran the course of the object, as if its stone skin had grown a glistening nervous system.

'It belongs to Varlos,' Gisella said in a trembling voice. 'We made our escape from the Darksmith Collective in this ship.'

Nicholas looked at her in wonder. 'Then you're truly from beyond the stars?'

'You could say that,' said the Doctor, peering past the cathedral-like spaceship into the near-blackness. 'And so is *this* thing.'

Frowning, Nicholas followed Gisella over to the Doctor to see what he meant. *Surely*, he thought, *nothing could surprise me now*? But his old legs trembled as he saw that the Doctor was pointing to *another* spaceship. This one was large and spiky, ringed with jagged metal turrets. The shell was chequered red and black like a poisonous creature warning the world away.

'Two different spaceships parked underground, right on top of each other,' the Doctor reflected. 'Doesn't seem very likely, does it?'

'I don't recognise the design,' said Gisella.

'Nor do I,' Nicholas whispered, as a horrible slithering noise started up in the darkness. *SSSCRAPE… SSSSSSCRAPE…* 'But I recognise that noise!'

The Doctor swung round to him. 'The vampire?'

'It's coming,' Nicholas croaked. 'And its not De Guerre…'

'Look!' Gisella screamed.

A dark, hideous creature had appeared from behind the spiky spaceship. Large, crimson eyes cast a blood-red glow over the rest of its tusked and twisted face. Its arms were long and sinewy, ending in misshapen pincers. Its legs were like rotten stumps protruding from the body of a giant slug. Round mouths stacked with teeth opened and closed all over its bloated body like baby birds hoping to be stuffed with food.

Frozen with terror, Nicholas watched the hideous creature come slithering over the rock to get them.

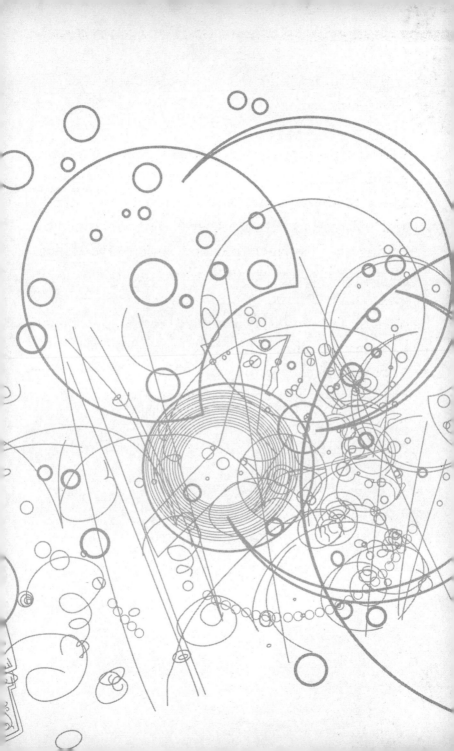

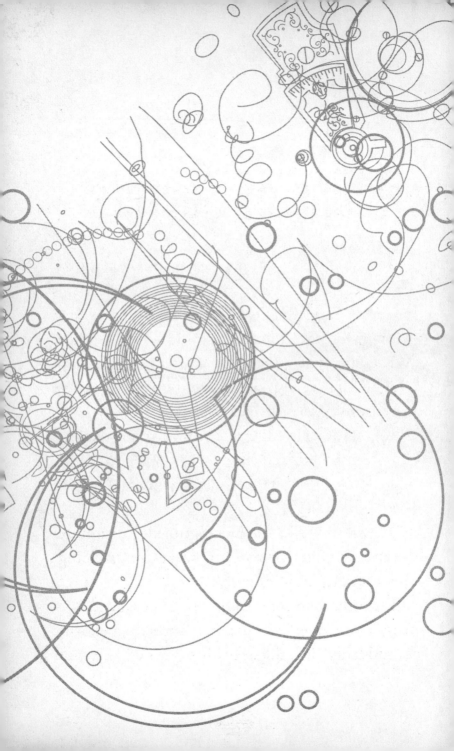

Ships of Secrets

Gisella shrank away, and Nicholas covered his eyes. But the Doctor actually took a step *towards* the vampire. 'Hello,' he breathed. 'What are you, then? A vortex dweller, am I right? It's a big old place but perhaps I've passed you once or twice…'

The black, glistening creature gave an obscene chuckle as it slithered closer.

'I don't think it feels like a chat, Doctor!' Gisella shouted.

'We *need* to talk,' the Doctor urged the vampire. 'I can't let you keep doing what you're doing. This stops, right now, or else—'

The time vampire raised its arms and all its many mouths jerked open in a screeching chorus, as suddenly its slug-like base reared up and

Activity

Predict the next symbols in each sequence to gain access to the ship?

1. ◉ ▣ ◎ ◎ △ ◎ ▣ ◎ ___

2. ⬠ ▣ ◻ △ ⬠ ◎ ⬠ ▣ ◻ ___

3. ▣ ◎ ◐ ▣ ◖ ◖ ▣ ◎ ◐ ▣ ___

it *flowed* across the rock towards the Doctor.

'Or else, I'll run away,' the Doctor concluded, turning and bundling Gisella and Nicholas behind the red and black craft. 'Right!' He held his oil lamp to the ship's surface. 'Door would be good. We're looking for a door.'

'But this must be the vampire's spaceship!' Gisella protested.

'That's right. If it won't give us answers, we'll have to find them for ourselves.'

'Look,' wheezed Nicholas. 'There's a kind of door here, I think…'

Gisella went to see. 'And an entry coder,' she said breathlessly. 'Simple pattern recognition.'

'Our vampire must think in pictures,' the Doctor realized. He pressed a button on the code panel and a small display screen lit up beside the door.

'…circle and no circle at all. An absence of circle!' The Doctor pressed his finger at the empty space on the screen and a steel shutter slid slowly open. 'Ha! *Molto bene*!'

The vampire was suddenly behind them, eyes blazing bright, multiple mouths snapping like piranhas.

'Get in!' Gisella urged them. Nicholas stooped with some difficulty and the Doctor wrestled him through the gap. Gisella darted inside through the Doctor's legs and then the Doctor followed, sonic screwdriver in hand. He fired a bright blue beam at the door and the shutter slammed shut again. Another sonic beam saw sparks fly from the wall and the door stayed shut.

Nicholas panted for breath. 'Are we safe?'

'I jammed the door,' the Doctor told him. 'For better or worse, we're trapped in here.'

Harsh white lighting flickered on, and Gisella looked around nervously. They were inside an airlock. The thick, metal inner doors stood open, and a blistered trail marked the floor.

'No guesses which way the vampire heads once it's inside,' the Doctor bounded off to explore. 'Come on!'

The lights rose and fell softly as they went, as if the whole ship were breathing in and out, waiting for something to happen. The corridors were wide and empty. The Doctor opened the nearest door.

'Cargo hold,' he said, looking round with interest.

Nicholas gasped as he stared upon a huge array

of twisted metal tubes studded with buttons and lights. To his eyes, they seemed merely weird, unsettling structures of glass and steel. But the Doctor understood their true purpose, and his face darkened.

'Weapons,' he breathed. 'Weapons from so many eras…'

'There's a good profit to be had, supplying guns from the future for conflicts in the past,' said a familiar voice behind them. 'Wouldn't you say?'

The Doctor, Nicholas and Gisella turned to find the gaunt figure of De Guerre watching them from the end of the corridor.

'Is that what you do?' the Doctor challenged him. 'Run guns for blood-hungry generals across time and space?'

'Hardly,' said De Guerre. 'But I understand how the chance of riches may turn a man to folly.'

'And these weapons,' the Doctor went on coldly. 'Is the time vampire one of them?'

'That unfortunate creature is merely the means of fuelling this vessel,' said De Guerre. 'The engines run on pure time energy, which the vampire collects from the nearest convenient source.'

Gisella nodded. 'The local population.'

'You mean…' Nicholas swallowed. 'My life was stolen by that beast to be used as… as power for generators?'

De Guerre nodded. 'It's all the poor thing knows how to do. He's just recharging his batteries.'

'What are you?' Gisella's eyes narrowed. 'Why do you keep the bones of a Darksmith in your dusty rooms? The bones of Varlos, my father!'

'Oh, my dear, precious child…' De Guerre smiled. 'The bones in the box were not those of Varlos. They belonged to the real De Guerre…'

Suddenly the old man's face began to shimmer. His features blurred and shifted. His hair thinned and disappeared. The black patch vanished. Two grey eyes now glowed like pearls in an ancient face lined with grave wisdom and translucent with age. Veins pulsed inside the gelatinous skin, and the bone structure of the skull itself was visible like a shadow inside the old man's face. The face of a Darksmith.

Gisella took a long, shuddering breath. 'Father?'

'Varlos,' the old man confirmed.

'So De Guerre died, and Varlos took his place.' The Doctor's face was stony. 'With the help of a little Darksmith magic.'

'Father, I don't understand.' The tears brimmed again in Gisella's eyes but still they would not fall. 'You tricked us, you kept yourself hidden… even from *me*.'

'With the Eternity Crystal involved, I could take no chances,' Varlos told her. 'I had to be certain why you and your companion had come here.'

'It's *your* motives I don't understand.' The Doctor slammed shut the door to the cargo hold. 'I mean, I can see why the great artist Varlos might come to Montmartre to live in the company of great artists, but why pose as De Guerre at all?'

'Baron De Guerre was the first victim of the time vampire,' Varlos explained. 'A regular visitor from the smart side of town, I believe he was besotted with a young hostess from the *Moulin Rouge*. I witnessed his murder… and once I learned the high regard with which De Guerre was held by the authorities, I saw a way to help bring an end to this sordid business as quickly and as quietly as possible.'

'Oh, Father…' Gisella ran and threw her arms around him. 'The Doctor brought me here through time. For you it's been barely weeks since you left – but for me, it's been so long, and I'm so glad that you're all right, that you *aren't* the killer. To know how brave you are...'

Varlos returned Gisella's embrace only briefly, then pulled away. 'It was not bravery that compelled me to fight,' he said grimly. 'It was fear. Fear that the vampire had been sent to destroy me. And when that seemed unfounded, I feared instead that its activities would draw attention to my being here.'

'So that's why you let DuPont believe his troubles were over when that poor animal was killed this morning,' the Doctor realized. 'If the truth of an alien time vampire got out there'd be a media circus worldwide. And this planet's just sending out its first radio waves, isn't it? Evidence of an alien presence bandied across the globe? Oh, you wouldn't want that. Not when you knew your Brothers in the Darksmith Collective would be scanning this part of the galaxy for any trace of you...'

'I knew they would come in the end.' Varlos stared at Gisella. 'But I never dreamed that you, of all people, would lead them straight to me.'

'It's not her fault.' The Doctor took hold

of Gisella's hand protectively. 'Your Eternity Crystal was discovered on the Moon, people started to die, I got involved – that's my story, now get on with yours. The vampire's right outside, between this spaceship and yours.'

'Bit of a coincidence, wasn't it?' Nicholas looked at Varlos. 'I mean, you're a spaceman and you somehow manage to land *under* Montmartre... and then another spaceship arrives next door.'

The Doctor took a step forward. 'Ah, but it wasn't coincidence, was it Varlos?'

Varlos lowered his head.

'*Was it?*' roared the Doctor.

'No.' The Darksmith's voice dropped to a dread whisper. 'I know that for certain now. Just as I know for certain that *I* am responsible for unleashing the vampire of Paris. The deaths, the horror and the carnage to come... it's all my fault, Doctor. *My* fault!'

Driven Out

'Save the self-pity for now,' said the Doctor quietly. 'Just tell us what you mean.'

Varlos nodded wearily. 'Come.' He turned and walked back down the corridor, and the Doctor, Gisella and Nicholas followed him into a sleek control room. The floor and walls were bare metal. Two elegant workstations sprouted from the floor, covered in buttons and dials. A large glass tank dominated the far wall, speckles of light and fire floating within in a mesmerising dance.

'Time engines,' the Doctor observed. 'Fully charged by the looks of it. Pretty crude technology – if the crew used a chronon filter, they'd get much better mileage…'

'Always so inventive, Doctor.' Varlos regarded

him. 'Your idea to construct a machine to trace the vampire's trail was inspired, so I attempted something similar with technology from my trunk this morning. But I soon found I needed more equipment.'

'So you had to go to your spaceship...' Nicholas was struggling to understand. 'And when you got here, you found this one alongside?'

'It must have come through in the same way I did,' Varlos agreed.

'What do you mean, "come through"?' said the Doctor

'When I fled the Darksmiths, I knew they would come searching.' Varlos explained. 'So I attempted to cover my tracks, travelling secretly to Earth through a small puncture in the space-time vortex, local to Paris...'

The Doctor nodded. 'Probably caused by some dodgy time experiments, ninety-odd years from now. I was there. Well, I *will* be there – oh, you know.'

'Whatever the cause, I took full advantage,' Varlos went on. 'With maximum shielding and a good deal of luck, I managed to steer myself safely through the hole in reality and landed here unseen.

But my passage through must have enlarged the fault considerably. It became a hazard.' Varlos gestured about him. 'It seems this craft ran aground on the fault as it travelled through the vortex.'

'The Agent came through it too,' said the Doctor. 'Didn't do wonders for him. How about the pilot of this thing, where is he?'

Varlos flicked a switch, and a black plastic couch slid out from one wall. Nicholas backed away as he saw a misshapen skeleton in leather coveralls sprawled on top of it.

'I found him dead. He must have perished with the rest of the crew. And so, while the ship's self-repair systems seem to have restored the ship, there's no one left to fly it.' Varlos's pale eyes held the Doctor's own. 'Don't you see? That is why the vampire – this beast of the vortex – roams the streets each night in search of fresh victims, gorging itself with raw time, straining its built-in shielding to breaking point.'

'It's following the only instructions it understands,' Gisella realized. 'But the time-engines are already full, and there's no one alive to siphon off the energy.'

'Right! But the vampire doesn't understand

that. It's thick and it's loyal and it's still following orders.' The Doctor was talking louder, faster. 'So the power builds and builds inside… It can't contain the load safely any more but on it goes, absorbing away but leaking energy as it does so – ever more violently, ever more unpredictably… Building up to a temporal explosion that could plunge half the planet back into Neanderthal times.'

'Or hurl it ahead into the far future,' Gisella added. 'Think of all those billions of lives blotted out, of the billions more who will never even be born…'

Nicholas was appalled. 'So what can you do about it?'

'Chronon filter!' The Doctor suddenly stood stock-still. 'That way of improving the drive systems I was talking about.'

'What about it?' said Gisella.

'The vampire's holding its stolen time energy in flux, right? Well, with a chronon filter we could separate the different temporal DNA patterns and if we could do that, maybe we could give *back* the stolen time to the vampire's victims!'

Nicholas's eyes were wide. 'You mean… I could be young again? My friends, too?'

'Don't raise his hopes, Doctor,' Gisella warned him. 'You've got to make a filter first.'

'Pretty much any ultra-sophisticated computer would do,' he shrugged. 'Well, with a bit of adapting.'

'But the time engines are already full,' she persisted, 'there's nowhere for the energy to go.'

'Yes, there is.' Varlos pulled something from his pocket – a large blue-white diamond, the size and shape of an egg. '*This* can store it until it can be safely dispersed.'

The Doctor stared. 'The Eternity Crystal? But how—'

'It is merely a replica I have prepared, not nearly as powerful,' Varlos confessed. 'I adapted one of my early prototypes. I thought perhaps I could switch it for the real Crystal – suitably booby-trapped of course. If nothing else it might be a useful bargaining counter if I was ever found.'

'Of course.' The Doctor snatched it. 'Well, if this thing *can* store the energy, all we need to do is find a way to channel it back to the original host bodies…'

Gisella raised her eyebrows. '*All?*'

The ship suddenly lurched as an explosion

tore through the corridor outside. The Doctor, Nicholas and Varlos were thrown to the floor, while Gisella fell against one of the workstations. Through the gusting smoke, she saw a familiar, gleaming figure come limping out of the ruined corridor towards them.

'The Agent!' she shouted. 'It must have found another way into the hillside. Father, it's tracked you down!'

'Sensors detect Brother Varlos,' the robot grated. 'And the Eternity Crystal is held in the Doctor's right hand.'

'Yep! And right in my hand is where it's staying,' called the Doctor.

The Agent raised its arm threateningly. 'Then, your hand shall be removed.'

'Been there, done that, thanks.' The Doctor jumped up. 'And anyway, one-handed, how could I do this?' He slammed one hand down on a control panel and pulled a lever with the other. A heavy shutter slammed down over the doorway, blocking the Agent from sight.

Gisella helped up Varlos. 'That won't keep it out for long, will it?'

'And now we can't get to the weapons in the

store,' Varlos realized, 'our best chance for stopping that thing.'

'How about we try using our heads?' The Doctor prowled about like a pinstriped panther. 'This is the control room, the most important room on the ship. There's got to be an escape pod or transference chamber or teleport or—'

'Or a door?' Nicholas offered. Still sprawled on the floor, he could see a high rectangle of hairline cracks in the metal beside the sparkling time engines.

'Nicholas, you should be a professional door spotter!' The Doctor hauled him to his feet. 'Ways in, ways out – he does them all!'

The shutter suddenly glowed dark red and began to smoke. 'The Agent does ways in too,' Gisella warned them.

The Doctor quickly used his sonic screwdriver to open the door and it slid back to reveal a short, dimly lit corridor. 'And off we go again!' he cried. Varlos set off first through the hatchway, then Gisella, then Nicholas and finally the Doctor. As they approached the end of the corridor, a shutter slid up to reveal the darkness of the cave outside.

'Direct escape route,' the Doctor realized. 'Useful for the crew in an emergency. As this would be.' He tapped a screen by the exit that displayed some kind of map. 'A plan of the terrain ahead.'

'We must hurry.' Varlos produced a small torch from his pocket and bathed the cave in bright blue light. Gisella joined him as he walked outside and cautiously checked the vessel. Nothing stirred in the torch beam.

'Perhaps the Agent killed the vampire,' Gisella suggested. 'Or scared it away, in any case.'

'I can sense it,' said Varlos darkly. 'It still lives.'

'Can we go back outside the same way we came?' Nicholas asked. 'We know the Agent is too big to get through.'

The Doctor tapped the screen. 'Looks like that way's been blocked by a rockfall. Our friendly neighbourhood Agent, presumably – cutting off our retreat.' There was a fresh clamour from the control room behind them. 'And here he comes now...'

Gisella ran back to the Doctor. 'We *must* find another route out of here.' She stared desperately at the map. 'If the Agent kills us while the vampire's still at large, he'll be condemning billions more to death! To go due east is shortest,' Gisella declared.

The Doctor pointed at the screen. 'But the south-easterly path takes us through these narrow paths *here*. That should slow up the Agent, buy us more time.'

'There is no time to be bought,' Varlos muttered. 'It will be getting dark soon. The vampire will feed again – and just one more victim could trigger the overload.'

A force beam spat out from the control room, scorching a black trail along the ceiling overhead. 'Run!' The Doctor pelted out into the blue gloom. 'This way!'

He led the way out of the vast cavern and through a winding maze of passages. Nicholas felt his old lungs crackle with every breath; but in the dark, it was easier to pretend he was nine again, and he willed himself to keep up. Luckily, Varlos couldn't move too quickly either. Trying not to trail too far behind the Doctor and Gisella, the two old men slipped and stumbled through the mined-out tunnels, past rusted scoops and abandoned trolleys, tripping over chunks of gypsum scattered across the floor like chunks of caked sugar. Every time they paused for breath, they heard the clanking and grinding of the robot Agent echoing eerily through the darkness behind.

They reached one of the narrow passes, where the tunnel dwindled to little more than a slit. Gisella helped them through while the Doctor checked the difficult passage ahead. 'We can make it,' he buoyed them. 'Not far now and we'll be out again in daylight.'

They had just squeezed through the second difficult pass, when the Doctor came to a stop so sudden that Gisella bumped into the back of him.

'What—?' she began, but he clamped a hand over her mouth.

'Up ahead,' he breathed, just loud enough for Nicholas and Varlos to overhear as well. 'The vampire!'

Varlos clicked off his torch. 'The beast has struck all over Montmartre, it must know every secret path to the surface.'

Holding still in the darkness, they could hear the creature's slithering, slug-like movement up ahead. For a moment Nicholas was transported back to the night when the creature had come to the orphanage. He had to fight the urge to turn and run blindly.

It was lucky he did. The next moment, the whole tunnel shook with incredible force and a white flash crackled through the darkness.

'The Agent's caught up!' the Doctor hissed. 'He's blowing open the passage behind us!'

Nicholas thought his old heart would finally stop as the vampire turned at the noise of the explosion, its crimson eyes like bloody gashes in the shadows of its face. It lifted its arms, howled and started creeping down the tunnel towards the group of four. And from the other direction came the clunk and clatter of the robot, tearing through the rubble to get to them.

Gisella clutched hold of Varlos. 'We're trapped!'

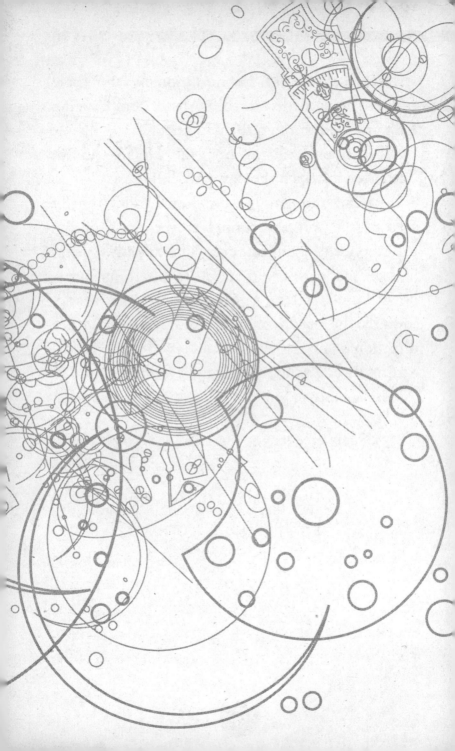

Chaos in the Caves

The Doctor clambered back to the narrow passage he and his party had just climbed through. 'Agent, stop!' he shouted. 'There's a creature here, riddled with unstable temporal energy. If your force beam strikes it—'

The Doctor was interrupted by another searing burst of light, and an explosion of shrapnel as the Agent started to widen the puckered mouth of the tunnel.

The Doctor scrambled back indignantly. 'You know, I don't think he believed me!'

The vampire was shuffling closer, its body undulating, its many mouths snapping and dribbling. The Agent fired again, the light ray knocking chunks not only from the fissure but also from the ceiling above them. Gisella cried out as a flurry of boulders narrowly missed her head.

'The robot is weakening the entire cave structure,' gasped Varlos.

'You're right.' The Doctor grinned wildly as he pulled out the sonic screwdriver. 'Perhaps we should give him a hand! Or some ultra-high frequency sound waves, anyway...'

The vampire howled, looming up mere metres away from them. The Agent unleashed another force beam from behind. Still larger chunks of rock were shaken loose from the fissure, and the whole passage was starting to shake. Through it all, the Doctor kept pointing the whirring screwdriver like a magic wand at the narrow pass. Dust and pebbles rained down around them.

'You could kill us all!' Varlos shouted.

'Or I could do nothing and these two will kill us anyway,' the Doctor snapped back. 'The vampire's trail of time-decay will have weakened this rock already. The Agent firing all over the shop will have weakened it further. So add a little more sonic resonating into the mix, and...'

'Too late!' Nicholas pointed to the Agent as it jammed its scarred metal body into the fissure in the rock. With a mechanical roar, it started to force itself through. The time vampire lifted its colossal, alien claws to strike out at the intruder but the Agent casually shot it, blasting the creature back into the shadows. Gisella shrieked and ran to Varlos, who grabbed her and held her close. The Doctor kept on with his sonic screwdriver, focusing the beam, apparently oblivious to anything else. Nicholas watched, terrified, as the Agent renewed its efforts to break through into their part of the passageway, ready to crush them all...

And then the ground collapsed beneath the robot's feet with an ear-splitting boom. One moment the Agent was there, the next it was plummeting from sight. The whole tunnel shook violently as a choking cloud of dust rose up from the inky blackness below. Then finally the tremors began to fade. Even so, Varlos kept a tight hold on Gisella, his back turned to the Doctor and Nicholas, staying in the shadows.

'There! That cave below us should be a good thirty metres deep.' Smiling, the Doctor switched off the sonic beam and stuck the screwdriver back in his pocket. 'Climbing back out should keep the Agent busy for a while.'

'But, Doctor,' Nicholas whispered. 'Look at the

vampire, it's *glowing*…'

The Doctor's smile dropped as he ran over to study the tusked monstrosity, lying on its back, wreathed in unearthly purple light. 'The energy backlash is starting,' he said hoarsely. 'The Agent's blast weakened the vampire's time shield beyond its tolerance levels. The pent-up time energy will be released at random.' He looked at the others. 'It's turned from a vampire into a time bomb, *literally* a time bomb.'

'How long have we got?' Nicholas asked desperately.

'Hours? Minutes? I don't know!'

Suddenly the vampire's eyes snapped open. Its mouths hissed angrily and its hideous tusked face twisted in pain. The rock it laid upon turned to dust as the monster rose up with a sucking, squelching noise.

'Back!' the Doctor ordered, jumping clear.

Snarling fearfully at the Doctor, as if believing him responsible for the pain it felt, the vampire slithered away into the darkness.

The Doctor stared after it helplessly. 'I have to get to the TARDIS and lash up a chronon filter. I'm a Time Lord, maybe I can use my own body as a conduit for passing back the time energy to the surviving victims.'

Varlos shook his head. 'To do that, you would need to join your consciousness to the Crystal matrix. Only a Darksmith brain can make that connection.'

'But a Darksmith body can't channel the raw time energy flowing out of the Crystal,' the Doctor retorted. 'You'd turn to dust.'

Varlos released Gisella from his embrace, and looked at her tenderly. Nicholas noticed one of the Darksmith tools was clasped in the old man's hand. 'Perhaps...' He smiled sadly. 'Perhaps there is another way.'

'Come on,' said the Doctor. 'We're close to one of the exit points unearthed by the excavations. The rockfalls must have felt like an earthquake to the people up above –let's just hope that they've cleared the streets and are hiding under tables. That vampire's unstable enough as it is, if it should feed again now...'

Gisella was the first away down the tunnel in pursuit. Her face was grave. She said nothing.

Nicholas and the Doctor followed her with Varlos bringing up the rear. Finally, weary, ragged and soaked with sweat, Nicholas heard the chitter of rats and saw a rectangle of daylight ahead in the darkness of the passage – the mouth of a storm drain.

And then he heard a young girl's screams from outside.

The Doctor and Gisella ran faster, leaving Nicholas and Varlos to keep up as best they could. The Doctor was first to reach the storm drain. As he wriggled out into the early evening light, he could almost feel time shift and shimmer about him. The street was packed with dozens of people as the vampire stood shivering in plain view. Some people shrieked in horror, some pointed and backed away, some were convinced this was some kind of artistic prank and were uncertain how to react.

The Doctor tried to give them a clue. 'Everyone back!' he bellowed.

But he was barely heard over fresh screams, as the vampire, its body blazing ever brighter, shambled desperately towards its final victims.

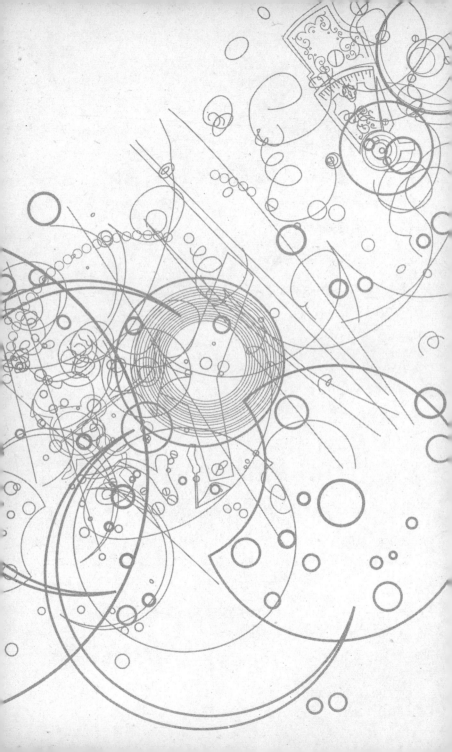

The Sacrifice

'**W**ait!' the Doctor shouted. Leaving Gisella by the storm drain he sprinted forward to bar the vampire's way. 'You must not do this. You understand me? Don't do this!'

The vampire snarled, but its eyes gazed curiously at the Doctor through the purple haze of energy.

'Yeah, you can feel it can't you? The weight of the centuries on me, the number of times I've died and come back.' The Doctor smiled sadly. 'I sometimes feel a bit of a vampire myself.'

'First an earthquake and now this? What is the meaning of this display!' Inspector DuPont came barging through the crowd towards the Doctor, red-faced with fury. The people quietened down to hear him. 'This is a celebration, for heaven's sake!'

The Doctor waved him back with one hand.

'And this is your vampire.'

'Nonsense,' DuPont insisted. But his face grew pale as he caught sight of the writhing, glowing creature. 'I've made it known, Doctor, that the people of this city are safe!' he hissed.

'Then make it known that you were wrong,' the Doctor snapped.

'Dead wrong.' Nicholas was scrambling out through the drain with a nine-year-old's enthusiasm, as Gisella looked on blankly. 'What of my friends, who aged close to death overnight!' he shouted, panting for breath. 'Are they joining your big party?'

DuPont looked uncomfortable. 'I'm having them brought to a retirement home on an autobus.'

'And is Madame Misra celebrating in her highchair?' Nicholas persisted.

'He is right, DuPont.' Now Varlos crawled out of the storm drain as DuPont frowned in amazement. 'There is a difference between protecting the people and tricking them, even if we believed our cause was just.'

'*Just* ran out of luck,' the Doctor quipped grimly, as the vampire began to flail about within its purple halo. 'The creature can't keep hold any longer.'

Nicholas stared helplessly as the vampire staggered back against a small lilac tree. In a burst of brightness the tree grew old and gnarled, its heavy flowers dissolved into dust. Fresh screams broke out as panic took the crowd. As if stung by his advisor's words DuPont waded in, appealing for calm, restoring order, helping to clear the area, even while wide-eyed with fear himself.

'The Crystal, Varlos!' the Doctor shouted. 'I'll have to risk connection and absorb all the energy I can, try to contain the blast.' He jabbed out his hand. 'Give it to me now!'

'Not luck, Doctor,' said Varlos calmly. 'I'll trust in my own handiwork, as I've always done.' He turned to Gisella, pressed the blue-pulsing gem into her hand and smiled sadly. 'Let us go together, my child.'

Wordlessly, Gisella ran with him and they hurled themselves towards the vampire creature.

'No!' yelled the Doctor, reaching out.

But he was too far away.

Too late.

Gisella and Varlos fell into the vampire's glittering haze. At once they became little more than shadows.

But the gem Varlos was holding glowed bright, like a blue eye searing away the haze, seeing everything. Gisella's black hair blew wildly as streaks of energy lashed out from her slender form into the slate-grey skies. Nicholas was struck by a bolt of her lightning and with a gasp, fell twitching to the floor. His body began to shine, to shrink in on itself…

And suddenly Nicholas was nine years old again, swamped in a second-hand suit.

'No filter, and still they processed the raw energy, sorted the temporal data…' The Doctor stared in wonder at the three figures in the haze of purple light, as the lilac tree shrank back into a flower above them. 'They gave all those living things their time back. But now, maybe it's time I broke things up…'

The Doctor reached into the haze and took Gisella and Varlos by the hand. As he did so, he joined their connection; his mind touched theirs, and through them he felt the pain of the vampire. It had known nothing but pain and loneliness and madness for so long. It was fading from sight, just a misshapen shadow now, its eyes shining with tears.

'Go,' the Doctor willed it. 'Back to the vortex. You'll be free at last.'

The shadow of the creature blew away in a last flare of light, melting into the empty air. Then it was gone.

Gisella and Varlos slumped to the ground and lay still. The Doctor knelt beside them. 'Gisella?' He felt for a pulse, but found none. She lay still, not breathing. Dark burns striped her forehead, and the skin had blackened and peeled away, and beneath...

Beneath he could see circuits and wiring, nano-relays, powerful transponder chips.

'Oh, Gisella,' the Doctor whispered. 'I said any ultra-sophisticated computer could act as a chronon filter. You had to go and prove it.'

'Yes, she did,' said Varlos weakly. 'Once I had made a few minor adjustments to her instinct programs, in the shadows.' He turned to look into the Doctor's eyes. 'I was not so much Gisella's father, as her creator.'

'She said she was suffering from an illness that kept her looking young,' the Doctor took the spent Crystal from her cold hand. 'But really she's a *robot*.'

'Far more that that, Doctor...' Varlos smiled. 'I conjured life... from metals and plastics... as I found my way to the Crystal's creation.' Specks of darkness were colouring his pearl eyes. 'I— I only saw the beauty in what I did, never the danger. But my work, today… it was good, yes? I saved lives. So much better… than saving the dead.'

The Doctor pushed the Crystal into his pocket and looked sadly at Gisella. 'Most of the time, I'd agree.'

'Gisella is *not* dead, Doctor. Her systems have simply crashed under the strain. They are restarting.' Varlos grabbed hold of the Doctor's wrist. 'But my time is over. You were right, of course, my body could not withstand the time energies as Gisella's could. Doctor, swear to me that you will destroy the Eternity Crystal. There is a way. You… you must…'

But the words died on Varlos's lips. His eyes closed. And then, with his last breath, his body faded away to nothing.

'*What* must I do?' the Doctor whispered.

'Is it over?' DuPont came forward cautiously. 'Doctor LeSmith, is the vampire finally destroyed?'

'Yes. It's gone,' the Doctor agreed. 'For real, this time.'

'All that we saw, it was like…' DuPont shrugged, still in shock. 'Like witchcraft and wizardry.'

'Am I dreaming?' Nicholas sat up, skinny, pink,

youthful – and grinning all over his face. 'Look! I'm me again!' He launched into a series of press-ups, then rolled over backwards, kicking his feet in the air. 'My body works properly! I can hear everything, see things clearly!' He broke off, frowning, as he noticed Giselle. 'Oh, no. Doctor, is she—'

Then Giselle sat up, coughing, shaking her head as if trying to clear it. The burns were already healing over.

'She's alive,' the Doctor confirmed, a grin spreading over his face. 'Oh, yes, she's very, *very* much alive!' He threw his arms around her and laughed. 'Witchcraft and wizardry, DuPont? Nah! It's magic and miracles you're seeing today! Magic and miracles for one day only! And where else would you see them but in Paris?'

Right on cue, a bunch of young boys in oversized clothes suddenly piled out of a horse-drawn bus and spilling excitedly into the road.

DuPont stared. 'The old men…?'

'Wa-heyy! The boys are back!' Nicholas shouted and ran to join his friends in wild jubilation. 'And here's to staying boys, as long as ever we can!'

'A day of miracles, it's true!' DuPont cried. He threw his cap into the air and himself into the noisy throng, dancing as a jazz band started to play. 'I want no more explanations, only *celebrations*...'

The Doctor laughed as the shell-shocked chief lost himself in the cavorting, carefree crowd. Then he turned to Gisella beside him.

'I saved everybody,' she told him, her eyes shining. 'Pierre Breton, the Missing Link... the woman turned to dust, Madame Misra... even the animals in the circus. They've all been restored.'

'But not your father,' the Doctor said sadly.

'For a few moments, Doctor, I was so close to him. Our minds touched. He showed me my soul.' She gave him a tearful smile. 'For the first time, I feel I know who I am – and who he was. I shall never forget him... even though it hurts.'

'If life didn't hurt now and again, we might as well be robots. And like Varlos said, you are so much more than that.' The Doctor helped her up, looked at the celebrating people of Paris as the moon rose over Montmartre. 'Come on. There's still a couple more things to do...'

An hour later, the TARDIS groaned back into existence beside the two spaceships hidden within the hillside. The Doctor left Gisella holding the real Eternity Crystal inside its small stasis casket while he went inside the red and black spaceship. Within minutes, he returned – and the spaceship vanished.

'Its engines were primed, so I sent it on its way,' he told her. 'Let it be a ghost ship, its guns lost forever, as it trails alone through the vortex…'

Gisella looked down at the casket in her hand. 'And you really think it will come?'

'Oh, yes,' said the Doctor. 'It'll never give up.' A clanking, grinding sound echoed to them from beyond Varlos's ship. 'Now, let's see if we can turn that to our advantage.'

'Doctor.' The robotic Agent appeared around the side of the Darksmith vessel. He was dented and scored with scratches, but still very much in one piece. 'Sensors indicate Varlos is dead. Return the Crystal or you shall join him.'

'You reckon?' The Doctor ushered Gisella and the Crystal inside the TARDIS while he stood defiantly in the doorway. 'Before Varlos died, he told us where we need to go to destroy the Eternity Crystal. We're off there now.' The Doctor waved as the Agent raised its fist, ready to fire. 'Bye-bye!'

He slammed the doors shut, which rattled under the force of the beam but didn't give way. Then he waited, crossing his fingers.

'What are you doing?' Gisella asked. 'Varlos didn't tell us how to destroy the Crystal.'

'No. But chances are the Agent knows how and where we could do it. And since he's got a lovely Darksmith ship right under his nose, he can head there now and try to stop us.' The Doctor grinned and flicked some switches on the TARDIS console. 'Not realizing that we will be following him. He'll lead us right to where we want to be!'

Gisella smiled. 'Doctor, that is extremely devious.'

'It is, isn't it!' the Doctor beamed. 'Aha! He's started the Darksmith engines. They'll just pop him through that little tear in reality and back out into local space...' He threw the take off lever and peered at the computer screen. 'We'll just wait for him in the Asteroid Belt, shall we? Look, here he comes...' But then the TARDIS lurched and shuddered. Sparks flew from the controls in a glittering shower. 'Oh, no...'

Gisella was thrown into the chair beside the

console. 'What's happening?'

'Varlos must have left a trap for anyone wanting to follow his ship. He's charged his slipstream with destronic particles.'

'That doesn't sound good!' Gisella yelled over the rising roar of the TARDIS' drive systems.

'A normal ship would burn up in a second.' The Doctor hung onto the console for dear life as the TARDIS spun and shook. 'Even with extrapolator shielding the particles will crack us open like an egg.'

'Then change course!'

'The controls are locked on.' He looked wildly at Gisella. 'If I can't get us free, we'll stay following that craft forever – in pieces!'

To Be Continued...

To find out what events lie in store
for the Doctor and the mystery of the
Darksmith Legacy, look out for
The Game of Death.
But for now, here is a taste of
things to come...

BBC

DOCTOR · WHO

Book
6

THE DARKSMITH LEGACY
THE GAME OF DEATH

BY TREVOR BAXENDALE

www.thedarksmithlegacy.com

Continue the amazing adventure online...

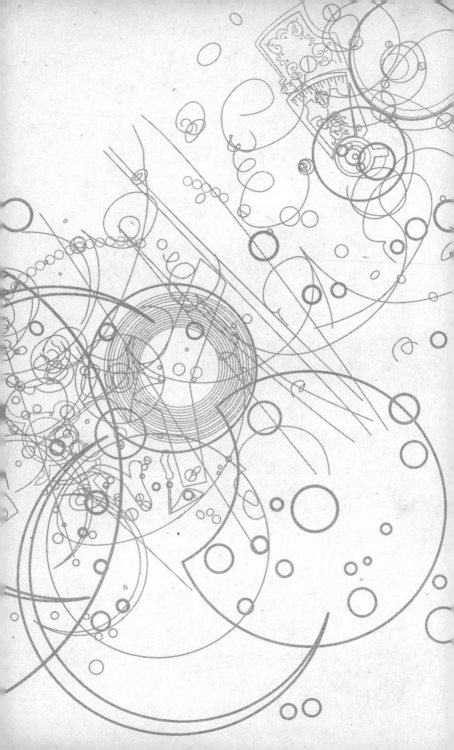

Crash Landing

The robotic Agent appeared around the side of the Darksmith vessel. He was dented and scored with scratches, but still very much in one piece. 'Sensors indicate Varlos is dead. Return the Crystal or you shall join him.'

'You reckon?' The Doctor ushered Gisella and the Crystal inside the TARDIS while he stood defiantly in the doorway. 'Before Varlos died, he told us where we need to go to destroy the Eternity Crystal. We're off there now.' The Doctor waved as the Agent raised its fist, ready to fire. 'Bye-bye!'

He slammed the doors shut, which rattled under the force of the beam but didn't give way. Then he waited, crossing his fingers.

'What are you doing?' Gisella asked. 'Varlos didn't tell us how to destroy the Crystal.'

'No. But chances are the Agent knows how and where we could do it. And since he's got a lovely Darksmith ship right under his nose, he can head there now and try to stop us.' The Doctor grinned and flicked some switches on the TARDIS console. 'Not realizing that we will be following him. He'll lead us right to where we want to be!'

Gisella smiled. 'Doctor, that is extremely devious.'

'It is, isn't it!' the Doctor beamed. 'Aha! He's started the Darksmith engines. They'll just pop him through that little tear in reality and back out into local space…' He threw the take off lever and peered at the computer screen. 'We'll just wait for him in the Asteroid Belt, shall we? Look, here he comes…' But then the TARDIS lurched and shuddered. Sparks flew from the controls in a glittering shower. 'Oh, no…'

Gisella was thrown into the chair beside the console. 'What's happening?'

'Varlos must have left a trap for anyone wanting to follow his ship. He's charged his slipstream with destronic particles.'

'That doesn't sound good!' Gisella yelled over the rising roar of the TARDIS' drive systems.

'A normal ship would burn up in a second.'

The Doctor hung onto the console for dear life as the TARDIS spun and shook. 'Even with extrapolator shielding the particles will crack us open like an egg.'

'Then change course!'

'The controls are locked on.' He looked wildly at Gisella. 'If I can't get us free, we'll stay following that craft forever – in pieces!'

More sparks flew from the TARDIS controls in a glittering shower. The Doctor was hanging onto the console for dear life now as the TARDIS tumbled through the Vortex, completely out of control. It was all the Doctor could do to stop himself being flung across the room.

'What's happening?' cried Gisella. She looked like a young, pretty girl with wide, dark eyes and black hair, but she was actually an extremely sophisticated android. She had been designed and built by a member of the Darksmith Collective, the galaxy's finest inventors. Gisella had joined the Doctor on his quest to destroy the ultimate weapon – the Eternity Crystal fashioned by the same Collective. But now Gisella found herself clinging onto the padded seats next to the

TARDIS console while the Doctor struggled with the controls, wondering if this trip through time and space would be her last.

The TARDIS engines groaned in protest as the ship plunged on.

'We've been caught in a temporal slipstream,' the Doctor said.

Gisella had no time to ask him what that could possibly mean before he grabbed a mallet from the underside of the console and gave the controls a mighty whack. Suddenly the TARDIS stopped heaving like a ship at sea and settled down.

The Doctor's face broke into a huge grin. 'There we are,' he announced. 'Never fails – when in doubt, hit it with a hammer!'

Cautiously, Gisella climbed down from the seat and approached the console. The Doctor was waving smoke away with one hand while he flicked switches and twisted dials with the other.

'Is it over?'

'What? Oh, that. Yeah, all done. The TARDIS and I know a thing or two about avoiding catastrophic time-space interstices.'

'You do?'

He nodded, but offered no further word of explanation.

The central glass column shone brightly, the internal filaments rising and falling. Gisella knew that this meant the TARDIS was still in flight. The Doctor was watching the hypnotic motion of the time rotor very closely, as if reading some significance in it as he made careful adjustments to the controls. 'Here we go,' he announced. 'Coming in to land...'

A raucous wheezing and groaning sound filled the room as the TARDIS began to materialise. Suddenly, the Doctor's cheery smile turned into an anxious frown.

'That can't be right,' he said as he grabbed the monitor screen and studied the readout.

'What's the matter?' Gisella asked. The strange tangle of information that filled the screen meant nothing to her – just a series of revolving hexagons and circles, like a digital schematic of the insides of a pocket watch.

'According to this we've materialised right in the middle of the Silver Devastation,' the Doctor said, frowning. He scratched his head in puzzlement. 'The TARDIS hung onto the Darksmith Agent's time trail without much difficulty – well, perhaps just a bit... all right, quite a lot of difficulty, actually – but these readings are all wrong. Very wrong.

DOCTOR · WHO

Fantastic free Doctor Who slipcase offer when you buy two Darksmith Legacy books!

Limited to the first 500 respondents!

To be eligible to receive your free slipcase, fill in your details on the form below and send along with original receipt(s) showing the purchase of two Darksmith Legacy books. The first 500 correctly completed forms will receive a slipcase.

Offer subject to availability. Terms and conditions apply. See overleaf for details.

re ─ ─ ─ ─ ─ ─ ─ ─ ─ ─ ─

Entry Form

Name: ....

Address: ....

Email: ....

Have you remembered to include your two original sales receipts? ◯

I have read and agree to the terms and conditions overleaf. ◯

Tick here if you don't want to receive marketing communications from Penguin Brands and Licensing. ◯

Important – Are you over 13 years old?

If you are 13 or over just tick this box, you don't need to do anything else. ◯

If you are under 13, you must get your parent or guardian to enter the promotion on your behalf. If they agree, please show them the notice below.

Notice to parent/guardian of entrants under 13 years old

If you are a parent/guardian of the entrant and you consent to the retention and use of the entrant's personal details by Penguin Brands and Licensing for the purposes of this promotion, please tick this box. ◯

Name of parent/guardian: ....

Terms and Conditions

1. This promotion is subject to availability and is limited to the first 500 correctly completed respondents received.
2. This promotion is open to all residents aged 7 years or over in the UK, with the exception of employees of the Promoter, their immediate families and anyone else connected with this promotion. Entries from entrants under the age of 13 years must be made by a parent/guardian on their behalf.
3. The Promoter accepts no responsibility for any entries that are incomplete, illegal or fail to reach the promoter for any reason. Proof of sending is not proof of receipt. Entries via agents or third parties are invalid.
4. Only one entry per person. No entrant may receive more than one slipcase.
5. To enter, fill in your details on the entry form and send along with original sales receipt(s) showing purchase of two Doctor Who: The Darksmith Legacy books to: Doctor Who Slipcase Offer, Brands and Licensing, 80 Strand, London, WC2R 0RL.
6. The first 500 correctly completed entries will receive a slipcase.
7. Offer only available on purchases of Doctor Who: The Darksmith Legacy books.
8. Please allow 31 days for receipt of your slip case.
9. Slip cases are subject to availability. In the event of exceptional circumstances, the Promoter reserves the right to amend or foreclose the promotion without notice. No correspondence will be entered into.
10. All instructions given on the entry form, form part of the terms and conditions.
11. The Promoter will use any data submitted by entrants for only the purposes of running the promotion, unless otherwise stated in the entry details. By entering this promotion, all entrants consent to the use of their personal data by the Promoter for the purposes of the administration of this promotion and any other purposes to which the entrant has consented.
12. By entering this promotion, each entrant agrees to be bound by these terms and conditions.
13. The Promoter is Penguin Books Limited, 80 Strand, London WC2R 0RL

Cut Here

Doctor Who Slipcase Offer

Brands and Licensing

80 Strand

London

WC2R 0RL